# THE PUPPY PLACE

# ROCKY

# THE PUPPY PLACE

**Don't miss any of these
other stories by Ellen Miles!**

# THE PUPPY PLACE

# ROCKY

ELLEN
MILES

## SCHOLASTIC INC.

New York   Toronto   London   Auckland
Sydney   Mexico City   New Delhi   Hong Kong

ISBN 978-0-545-34836-2

Cover art by Tim O'Brien
Original cover design by Steve Scott

12 11 10 9 8 7 6 5 4 3 2 1          12 13 14 15 16 17/0

Printed in the U.S.A.                                    40

First printing, January 2012

*For Ellie, Emily, and J.D.*

# CHAPTER ONE

Dear Allyson,

Hi, how are you? My name is Lizzie Peterson. I'm in fourth grade at Littleton Elementary School. My teacher, Mrs. Abeson, is the one who came up with this pen-pal project. She is super-nice and never, ever yells. My best friend, Maria, is in my class. She and I have a dog-walking business. I have two brothers, both younger. Their names are Charles and the Bean (well, his real name is Adam). They are both okay, I guess, though some-times annoying. My dad is a firefighter and my mom is a newspaper reporter. We have a puppy named Buddy — he is the BEST . . .

Lizzie dropped her pencil and reached down to scratch Buddy between the ears. He loved that. When she stopped, he pushed against her hand for more. Buddy really was the best. He was a mutt, small and brown with a heart-shaped white spot on his chest, and Lizzie could not possibly love him any more than she did. He was the sweetest, cutest puppy ever — and Lizzie had known a lot of sweet, cute puppies. That was because her family fostered puppies: they took care of puppies who needed homes, just until they found the perfect forever family for each one.

Fostering puppies was exciting and fun and also hard work. Sometimes it was really sad, like when they had to give up a puppy they'd fallen in love with. But Lizzie loved it. She loved how each puppy had his or her own personality. She loved playing with the puppies and helping train them. And she loved finding them homes.

She looked down at the letter she had started. She would have to tell Allyson, her new pen pal, all about fostering puppies. But first, couldn't she make her letter a little more interesting? She wanted to be the kind of pen pal someone would want to write to for years and years, like Mrs. Abeson's pen pal.

Her teacher had told the class all about Marisol, the pen pal she had started writing to when they were both ten years old. Marisol lived in Spain, and her father was a bullfighter! Thirty years later, Marisol and Mrs. Abeson still wrote to each other, and they had visited each other many times. That was why Mrs. Abeson had decided that their class should have a pen-pal project.

Earlier that week, during Language Arts,

Mrs. Abeson had picked pen-pal names out of a hat. She read out the name of a boy or girl for each boy or girl in Lizzie's class. Lizzie had squeezed her eyes shut hard and wished for a girl her age who lived in an exotic place, like New Zealand or Ecuador. Her wish had come true — at least, sort of, when Mrs. Abeson had told her that her new pen pal would be Allyson, a girl in fourth grade who lived on a sheep ranch in Montana.

Maria, Lizzie's best friend, had also gotten a girl pen pal. Her name was Becky, and she lived in Kansas. BOR-ing!

Lizzie looked at her letter again. What if Allyson, her new pen pal, thought *she* was boring? She needed to jazz things up a little. She would probably never meet Allyson, and even if she did it would be *years* from now. Why not

4

make herself, and her life, sound a little more interesting? She started her letter again.

Dear Allyson,

My name is Lizzie, but my friends call me Sarabeth. I have two younger brothers, named Sebastian and Wolfgang, and an older sister named Delicata. She is very beautiful. My father is the fire chief in our city, and my mother is editor of the newspaper. We have five dogs: a puppy named Buddy and four older dogs named Henry, Beezus, Ramona, and Ralph. We also have three cats, two turtles, a guinea pig, and several hamsters. For my next birthday I might get a llama . . .

Lizzie smiled. That was more like it! Allyson was going to be thrilled to have such an interesting, exciting pen pal. "What do you think, Buddy?" Lizzie asked. She sat down on the kitchen floor and pulled him into her lap. Then she read her letter to him. It sounded even better when she read it out loud.

The letter wasn't done yet, though. Mrs. Abeson had said they should tell their pen pals about themselves and their families, but also about their daily lives. "Look at the newspaper," she'd suggested. "Tell your pen pal about a current event, so he or she can get a picture of what life is like here in Littleton."

Lizzie got up and went into the living room to find the paper. Buddy followed her, trotting along with his ears perked and his tail held high. He was always happy to see what happened next — that was one of the things Lizzie loved best about him.

Buddy went straight for his toy basket and

pulled out Mr. Duck. He chewed on the stuffed bird's belly to make it squeak, then tossed it up in the air and raced to pounce on it when it fell. He made it squeak some more, then trotted over to Lizzie to show off his prize.

"Very nice," Lizzie said. "Good dog, Buddy." But she wasn't really paying attention. She was reading through the paper, trying to find something — *anything* — interesting to tell Allyson about. There wasn't much. Littleton was not a very exciting town, and Saturday's paper was always especially boring. The main headline was about a school board meeting, and Lizzie's mom had written an article on the second page about a ground-breaking ceremony for the new soccer field at the recreation center. Lizzie looked through every single page of the *Littleton News* without finding one single interesting thing to tell Allyson. Maybe she would have to make something up. She thought about that as she glanced over the classified ads in the back.

What could she say? Maybe she could tell Allyson that a sports or movie star was coming to live in Littleton. Or what about writing that a meteorite had crashed to Earth in the middle of town, or that a bear had attacked someone in the park?

Then Lizzie saw something that made her eyes open wide. Instantly, she forgot all about Allyson, meteorites, bears, and sports stars. It was right there, in the middle of the classifieds, under the heading *Pets*. A tiny ad, with a bold headline: FREE PUPPY.

# CHAPTER TWO

Lizzie caught her breath and took a closer look. *Free Puppy*, the ad said. *Bulldog.* Then there was a phone number. That was all.

She frowned. Why didn't it say "To a Good Home"? It sounded like they were just going to give the puppy to the first person who called. That wasn't right. Ms. Dobbins, the director of the local animal shelter where Lizzie volunteered every week, would never do that. If someone wanted to adopt a pet from Caring Paws, they had to fill out a long application with lots of information about who they were, where they lived, and how they planned to take care of the animal that was about to become part of their family. Ms. Dobbins didn't let just anyone walk in, pay the adoption fee, and walk back out with a cat or dog.

Lizzie's aunt Amanda, who ran a doggy day-care center where Lizzie sometimes helped out, would have agreed. She had told Lizzie that responsible dog breeders never sold puppies without interviewing buyers first.

Lizzie thought for a second. Then she closed the notebook in which she'd been writing her pen-pal letter. She picked up the newspaper and pushed back her chair. "Mom!" she yelled.

Buddy scrabbled to his feet and followed her out of the kitchen and up the stairs.

"Mom," Lizzie said again as she walked into her mother's study.

Mom spun around on her office chair and rubbed her eyes. "What is it, honey?" she asked.

She looked tired. Mom had been working hard lately on a series of articles called "Exceptional Elders," about interesting older people in the community. So far she had interviewed a farmer, a husband-and-wife team who ran a flower shop, and a retired detective. She said she loved the project, but Lizzie had noticed that she often went back into her study late at night, instead of reading or watching a movie in the living room.

"Mom, look at this ad." Lizzie plopped the paper down on her mother's lap.

Mom picked it up and studied the classifieds. "Which one?" she asked. "The one where someone's selling a saltwater aquarium? I don't think we —"

"No, this one." Lizzie pointed to the ad.

"Aha," said Mom. "Well. I hope they find the puppy a good home."

"Exactly," said Lizzie. "That's exactly my point. It doesn't even look like they're trying!" She picked up the paper. "It's like they don't care *who* takes the puppy."

Mom nodded. "That's too bad," she said.

"Mom?" Lizzie went over to lean on her mom's chair. Buddy joined her, leaning against Mom's legs.

"Oh, no, Lizzie. You're not thinking —" Mom started to shake her head.

"I am," said Lizzie. "I think we should foster this puppy. We haven't fostered a puppy since Cocoa." True, Cocoa had been a bit of a challenge. The chocolate Lab had been so full of energy. Maybe it was better not to talk too much about Cocoa. Lizzie changed the subject. "Plus, I've always wanted to foster a bulldog. They're so cute, with their grumpy, wrinkly faces and their short little legs."

Mom let a smile slip. "They are cute," she admitted. "My friend at work has a mug with a picture of a bulldog on it. It's hilarious."

"So? Can't we at least call?" Lizzie was dying to meet the giveaway pup. "You know we would do a better job of finding this puppy the perfect home." Lizzie snuggled up closer to her mom. "Please?" she asked, in her sweetest voice. "Charles and I will take care of the puppy."

Mom sighed. "I have to admit that you have both been very responsible with all our foster puppies."

Lizzie held her breath and crossed her fingers. Buddy put a paw on Mom's lap. "Well, I suppose we could call and find out more," said Mom.

Lizzie let out a whoop and threw her arms around her mother. "Yes!" she cried. "A bulldog puppy! I can't wait." Buddy jumped up and danced a crazy little happy-dance, squirming all over with joy.

"Lizzie," Mom warned, "I didn't promise —"

"I know, I know," said Lizzie. She went over to grab the phone. "You just said we could call. So let's call. Now. Can we? Please?"

Mom shook her head. "Elizabeth Maude Peterson. You are a champion wheedler, did you know that?" But she was smiling. She took the phone and began to dial. Then she hesitated. "I should at least *talk* to Dad before I call," she said.

"He'll be okay with it," Lizzie said. "You know he will. He always is. He loves all the puppies we foster." This was true, although there were probably a few puppies he loved a tiny bit less than others, like Chewy and Chica, the troublesome Chihuahuas.

"You're right," said Mom. "Anyway, he and the

boys are at the ice arena. He'd never be able to hear me over the noise of the hockey game."

"Exactly." Lizzie picked up the newspaper and pointed to the number in the ad. "Come on, let's call." She read out the number.

Mom dialed. "Yes, hello," she said when someone answered. "Is this the person who advertised the free puppy?" Lizzie's heart began to beat like a tom-tom drum.

# CHAPTER THREE

Lizzie wanted to jump up and down. She wanted to shout. She wanted to dance around the room. This was so exciting! But she wanted to hear every word of what Mom was saying, so instead she plopped down on the floor and pulled Buddy into her lap. She buried her face in his neck as she listened to Mom's half of the conversation.

"The puppy is a bulldog?" Mom asked. She knit her brow and nodded. "Uh-huh, uh-huh, I see," she said. "And so you want to find him a new home."

Him! Lizzie grinned. The puppy was a boy. A boy bulldog. She couldn't wait to meet him. He must be totally adorable.

"Well, our family fosters puppies, and we thought maybe —" Mom stopped, listening. "You would? Right now?" She put a hand over the receiver and turned to Lizzie. "He said he'd like us to come meet Rocky," she said.

"Rocky?" Lizzie jumped to her feet. "His name's Rocky? That's so totally, completely, absolutely perfect for a bulldog. Yes, tell him yes! Let's go!" Now she couldn't help it. She *had* to dance. She twirled and spun all around Mom's chair. "Rocky! Rocky! Rocky the bulldog!" she sang. Buddy jumped up again and danced around with her, wagging his tail and grinning a doggy grin.

Mom frowned at her and put a hand over her

free ear so she could hear what the person on the other end was saying. "Okay, so it's the second left, then up the hill, and your store is on the right side of the street?" She reached for a pen and scribbled down the directions. "Well," she said finally, "I guess we can be there in" — she checked her watch — "about half an hour? Will that be okay?"

Lizzie was about to burst. And when Mom hung up, she did. "Rocky!" she yelled, loudly enough that Buddy got all excited and started to bark.

Mom put both hands over her ears. "Lizzie," she said. "I can't hear myself think. Calm down."

"Calm down?" said Lizzie. "How can I calm down? We're getting a bulldog puppy! Right now!"

Mom smiled. "Tell you what. Go downstairs and take Buddy out in the backyard before we go.

Run around a little and blow off some of that steam, would you? I just have to write one more e-mail. And I'll try to call Dad to let him know what's up. Then we'll go."

Lizzie clattered down the stairs with Buddy bounding beside her. She banged out the back door. "Whoopee!" she yelled as she and Buddy tore around the yard.

Mom was right, as usual. Running around helped, and Lizzie did feel a little calmer by the time she climbed into the van and buckled her seat belt. "So, where are we going?" she asked. "Where does Rocky live?"

"He lives at a store," Mom said. "Albert's Electronics. The man I talked to — his name's Albert Lowell — owns the place."

"A store?" Lizzie asked. "What do you mean?"

"Well, Mr. Lowell lives at the store, too," Mom

explained. "I guess he has an apartment upstairs. But the point is, he got Rocky because he felt he needed a guard dog. Some stores near him have been burglarized recently. But —"

Lizzie laughed. "I bet I can guess!" she said. Lizzie prided herself on knowing everything there was to know about dogs. Every night she studied her "Dog Breeds of the World" poster, and she practically had it memorized. "Bulldogs might look mean and ferocious, but they're not. Stubborn, maybe. But not scary. Most of them are actually sweet little pooches who love to be around people. I hear they can be real clowns, too."

Mom looked at Lizzie in the rearview mirror. "You really are something else, my girl," she said. "You hit the nail right on the head.

That's exactly what Albert said. He said Rocky wouldn't bark at a stranger if the person were carrying three TVs and a stereo system out of the store."

"So he wants to get rid of him?" Lizzie asked. "That seems mean, just because he's not cut out to be a guard dog." She felt bad for Rocky.

"I guess Albert also found out that he's not really a dog person," Mom said. "He's going to install an alarm system instead. When I told him we foster puppies, he jumped at the chance to give Rocky to someone who could find him the right home." Mom squinted up at a road sign. "Does that say 'Terrace Street'?" she said. "I think this is where we turn."

Lizzie didn't answer. She was thinking about this guy Albert. Why did people get dogs if they weren't going to love them and keep them forever?

A few minutes later, Mom pulled up in front of a yellow building. "This is it," she said. "There's the sign: Albert's Electronics."

Lizzie folded her arms. "I'm going to wait out here," she said.

Mom turned to look at her. "What? I thought you'd be dying to meet Rocky."

"I am," Lizzie said. "But I'm not so sure I want to meet this guy Albert. I feel kind of mad at him, and I might not be able to hide it. He acts like a dog is like a CD player, or a toaster, or — or just something you can toss away if it's not living up to your expectations."

Mom nodded. "Okay," she said. "I understand. I'll go in on my own."

Lizzie waited in the van, arms folded, feeling angrier by the minute. But her anger fell away when she saw Mom come out the door, carrying a white puppy with brown and black splotches. Lizzie threw open the door of the van. "Rocky!" she said.

The puppy looked up at her, his funny flat face wrinkled with curiosity.

*How do you know my name?*

Lizzie held open her arms, and Mom leaned in to put Rocky on her lap. The puppy was surprisingly heavy, and his short fur was soft. His head seemed huge, and his droopy jowls made him look like a wise old man. He had a big, flat, wrinkly face; broad shoulders; a wide, muscular chest; and short, stocky legs. His stubby tail wagged hopefully as he looked up at Lizzie. He snorted and licked her hand as she petted him. He was a funny-looking little thing, just adorable. "Hello, you silly boy," Lizzie murmured as she petted him. Rocky sighed and settled into her lap.

The puppy was asleep by the time Mom buckled in and started the van.

And he was snoring loudly by the time she turned back onto Terrace Street.

# CHAPTER FOUR

"You know," Mom said, as she drove toward home, "this Albert person really was not such a bad guy. I think he just got in over his head. He had no idea how much responsibility it is to own a dog."

Lizzie put a hand on Rocky's head. "Still," she said. "Didn't he care at all about where Rocky ended up?"

"He did," Mom said. "He told me he was planning to have a long talk with anybody who called. He was going to ask the right questions, about whether they'd had a dog before and how they planned to care for a puppy. All that stuff."

Lizzie sniffed and looked out the window. "Well, that's good." She still wasn't so sure about Albert Lowell, but what did it matter anymore? "We've got you now," she whispered into Rocky's little rosebud-shaped ear. He snorted in his sleep, and his ear twitched. Lizzie smiled. Now the Petersons were fostering this puppy, and that meant they would keep him safe and sound and happy until they could find him the perfect forever home. "Right, Rocky?" Lizzie whispered again. Rocky answered with a long, loud snore.

When they pulled into the driveway, Dad's red pickup was there, too. "They're home," said Lizzie. "Wait 'til everybody meets Rocky!" She made sure the puppy's leash was clipped on, and led him out of the van and into the front yard.

Rocky snuffled and sniffed his way up the walk, stopping to investigate each blade of grass and every tulip. Lizzie tried to keep him moving, but Rocky was stubborn. And he was strong. He was not a big puppy, but he was all muscle. When Lizzie pulled on the leash, he just set his short, squat legs and pulled back harder.

*Who's the boss here? Don't rush me!*

Lizzie laughed. She could be stubborn, too. But for today, at least, she decided to let Rocky have his way. After all, it was his first day in a new place, with a new family. She stood patiently as he snorted and snuffled. His flat, wrinkly face was so cute, and she loved the way his jowls shook when he found an especially interesting smell.

The front door opened. "What have we here?" Dad asked, poking his head out. "Is this the famous Rocky that Mom called me about?"

"Rocky!" said Charles from behind Dad. He and the Bean pushed their way past their father and ran outside to meet the new puppy. Buddy followed them, running headlong toward Rocky, his tail wagging and his eyes bright.

Rocky looked up just in time to see them all coming at him. His eyes grew wide. He tilted his head at Lizzie, wrinkling his forehead.

*More people? And a dog?*

Quickly, Lizzie scooped him up. "Slow down, guys," she told her brothers. "Give him a chance to get to know you." She tightened her arms around Rocky. He was awfully heavy to hold. In fact, he was sort of sliding down her legs. Charles zipped over to give him a boost.

"He's cute," said Charles. "What a funny face."

The Bean reached up to pet Rocky. "Hi, uppy," he said. "Nice uppy."

"Easy," Lizzie said. "Remember, he's a new dog. We don't really know him yet." But she was just about positive that Rocky would never nip or growl at anybody. She'd only known him for a few minutes, but she could already tell he was a total pussycat. No wonder he had not worked out as a guard dog.

Buddy circled around Lizzie's knees, panting with excitement. Rocky did not seem afraid, so with a sigh of relief, Lizzie let him back down. He and Buddy sniffed each other, tails wagging.

Then Buddy put his front paws down and his rear end up and gave Rocky a big doggy grin.

*Wanna play?*

Rocky lay down and rolled over onto his back, paddling his paws in the air. His jowls fell back so that it looked as if he wore a huge smile. Lizzie and the rest of her family cracked up. "That is hilarious," said Charles.

Then Rocky rolled back over and ambled his bowlegged way on up the walk, continuing his sniffing and snuffling.

Dad grinned. "What a little tank," he said. "He doesn't look like the world's most active dog."

"No," said Lizzie. "He's sweet, though."

Inside, everybody helped get Rocky settled. Charles set up the dog bed that they used for foster puppies, and Mom put out the extra food and water dishes. Lizzie and the Bean showed Rocky where the dog toys were kept in the basket in the living room. Rocky did not seem too interested in any of the stuffed toys, but he did sniff at a squeaky plastic hot dog. Then he turned and put one paw on the couch, ready to try to climb up.

"I don't think so, champ," said Dad, gently pushing him back down. "In this house, couches are for people."

Rocky wrinkled his nose and looked up at Dad.

*You're kidding, right?*

Lizzie laughed and called Rocky into the kitchen. "Come sit here with me, you silly," she said, hauling him onto her lap. She needed to finish up her pen-pal letter and get it into the mail. She pulled her letter out of her notebook and began to copy it over. She used her best stationery, the notepaper Aunt Amanda had given her, with pictures of puppies around the borders. When she was done, she would address the envelope and put on a bunch of dog stickers.

Before she had even finished the first paragraph, Rocky was asleep on her lap.

# CHAPTER FIVE

"I wonder when we'll get letters back from our pen pals," said Lizzie on Monday afternoon.

"Daphne Drake already heard from hers," Maria said. "She sent her pen pal her e-mail address, and they've been writing back and forth a bunch already."

Lizzie wished she had thought of that. She was impatient for her first letter from Allyson.

School was over, and Lizzie and Maria were finishing up their dog-walking for the day. They were partners in a business called AAA Dynamic Dog Walkers, and it sure did keep them busy. Every day after school they headed out together to walk dogs. It took a while since they had a lot of clients. They could each handle two dogs at a time, though it wasn't always easy. Every dog got at least a twenty-minute walk, and Lizzie also usually threw in some free training. She had taught three of the dogs to shake hands, and one of them was even learning how to roll over.

They had already walked Tank, Pickle, Atlas, and Molly, their most active and energetic charges. Then they'd taken Dottie the Dalmatian out; she didn't get along as well with the other dogs. Plus, she was deaf and only responded to hand signals, so it was easier to walk her on her own.

Now they were walking Ginger, who Lizzie liked to call The World's Pokiest Dog. Or rather, Maria was walking Ginger. Lizzie held

Rocky's leash. He needed a walk, too, and Lizzie had figured that Ginger was just about Rocky's speed. Usually it took the whole twenty-minute walk just to get Ginger around the block. You spent half of that time pulling on her leash and begging her to keep moving. Some days, once you got her a certain distance away from her house, she would stop trying to plod back home and might even become interested in trying out a new block, in a new direction.

Today was not one of those days. "I knew Ginger was a slowpoke, but this is ridiculous," Lizzie said to Maria.

"Well, Rocky's not helping any," Maria said. "In fact, I think there may have to be a new entry in the Guinness book under 'World's Pokiest Dog.'" She gave a gentle tug on Ginger's leash and rolled her eyes when the basset mix tugged back, standing her ground. "At least Ginger has an excuse. She's old. But Rocky's a puppy."

Each dog sniffled and snuffled at a different side of a big bush at the end of someone's driveway. Rocky's big brown eyes were bright in his flat, wrinkled face as he snorted. He pawed at the bush.

"Rocky," Lizzie said, giving his leash a little pull, "you've been sniffing that bush for about fifteen minutes. Can we go now?" She sighed. "I've been trying everything to get him going," she told Maria. "I've never seen such a couch potato. Remember when we fostered Muttley? He was lazy, but at least he usually slept with one eye open so he could look over everyone. Rocky just snores. I don't think he'd notice if a freight train came roaring through the house."

"I guess that's why he's not a good watchdog," said Maria. "Does he ever bark?"

Lizzie shook her head. "I've only heard him bark once, when he found Buddy sleeping in his favorite spot. I thought maybe I could teach him to bark, so Albert Lowell would take him back, but so far that hasn't worked."

"How do you teach a dog to bark?" Maria asked.

"Good question," Lizzie said. "I tried to look it up in all my dog training books, but they only had information on how to teach a dog *not* to bark. So I just figured I would reward him for barking, by giving him a treat when he does it. But since he never barks . . ."

"He never gets the treat," said Maria. "Okay, so watchdog is off the list. I guess you have to figure out what else Rocky might be good at."

"You mean, besides that?" Lizzie pointed at Rocky, who had decided to roll over and paddle his paws in the air while he waited for Ginger to finish sniffing. She and Maria cracked up. Rocky opened one eye to glare at them.

*Can't a puppy get some rest around here?*

He paddled his paws some more. His wrinkled face and flappy jowls looked especially funny upside down. Rocky seemed to like making the girls laugh. He squirmed and grinned at them, blinking lazily.

"Maybe he could be a clown," suggested Maria. "Doesn't Charles's friend David have a cousin who's in the circus?"

Lizzie nodded. "Right," she said. "Charles thought that guy might adopt Sweetie." Sweetie was a miniature poodle the Petersons had fostered. She was great at tricks. "But Sweetie was like a little jumping bean. She was full of energy and always up to something. Rocky — well, he has a few crazy spells every day when he acts silly and makes me laugh, but besides that . . ." She looked down at the bulldog pup, who was sprawled out on the sidewalk like a rug. She shrugged. "I don't think the circus is in Rocky's future."

"Probably not search and rescue, either," Maria said with a giggle. Scout, a German shepherd the Petersons had fostered, was already learning how to find lost people and save their lives.

"Or agility," said Lizzie. She thought of Flash, a border collie puppy who was quicker than lightning. He was perfect for the sport of agility, where dogs clambered up and over tall A-frames, galloped through tunnels, and flew over jumps.

"Can you imagine Rocky lumbering around an agility course?" By now, both girls were laughing.

Rocky rolled over onto his feet and started his slow amble again, tugging Lizzie along with him as he headed to the next bush for a big sniff. Lizzie sighed. How was she ever going to find the perfect owner for this slowpoke pup?

# CHAPTER SIX

"I got a letter! I got a letter!" Maria came running up the sidewalk waving an envelope.

It was Thursday after school. That meant it was dog-walking time again. Lizzie waited outside Maria's house with Atlas, the golden retriever. She and Maria were about to pick up Tank, a young German shepherd. But first, they had stopped at Maria's house to see if she'd gotten mail from her pen pal.

"Let's see," Lizzie said, reaching out for the envelope. Why hadn't *she* gotten a letter yet? Three other people in their class had heard back from their pen pals already, and now Maria had gotten a letter, too. It wasn't fair.

"Wait, I didn't even open it yet," Maria said, pulling it back.

A little corner of the envelope ripped and Lizzie ended up holding a scrap of paper. "Oops," she said. "Sorry."

But Maria barely noticed. "Did you see all the horse and pony stickers on the envelope?" she asked. "And look, she has horse stationery, too! We have a lot in common."

Maria loved horses as much as Lizzie loved dogs. Lizzie wondered if Allyson, her pen pal, was a dog lover. She hoped so. Maybe they could trade stickers. That is, if Allyson ever wrote back.

Maria started to read out loud as she and Lizzie walked up to the door of the house where Tank lived. "It says, 'Dear Maria, I'm glad we get to be pen pals! We have so much in common —'" Maria stopped and grinned at Lizzie. "That's exactly what I just said!"

Lizzie grinned back. But she felt a little twinge in her tummy. So, was this Becky person going to turn into Maria's new best friend or something? Lizzie reached up to knock on the door. A blast of barking broke out inside. "Hush up, Tank!" yelled a voice. Then, "He's all ready for you," the voice added.

Lizzie opened the door and Tank came barreling out. She grabbed his leash as he tried to bolt past her. "Whoa, there, pal," she said. Luckily, Tank's owner knew that the big shepherd pup needed to wear a special head halter, since a plain old collar would never be enough to control him. Tank and Atlas greeted each other with happy sniffs and wagging tails. "Want me to walk both dogs so you can read your letter?" she asked Maria.

Maria nodded happily. "Just for a few minutes, okay?" They headed down the street, following their usual route. Maria held the letter in front of her as she walked. "'I live on a farm in Cherokee County,'" she read out loud, "'with my mom and my dad and my uncle Bob. I have a sister named Martha. We have seventeen goats, a hundred and two cows, and a bunch of chickens and ducks. Also my dad raises corn and soybeans.'"

Lizzie smiled. Becky didn't really sound so boring after all. Still, Allyson just *had* to be more interesting than that. If she ever wrote.

Tank and Atlas dragged Lizzie along. They

were both young, energetic dogs and together they were like a team of horses pulling a sleigh. Atlas, especially, reminded Lizzie of Cocoa, the chocolate Lab puppy. Cocoa was so full of energy that she had galloped into her owner and knocked him over. Judge Thayer was okay now — in fact, he was one of the people Lizzie's mother was interviewing for her Exceptional Elders series — but he and his wife, Charlotte, had agreed that they were getting a little too old and frail to take care of a dog like that. Luckily, the Petersons had found the perfect home for Cocoa. Lizzie would have to tell Allyson that whole story next time she wrote to her.

"Lizzie, are you listening?" Maria poked Lizzie in the side. "Did you hear the part I just read about the calf that Becky is raising as a Four-H project?"

Lizzie nodded. She had been listening. Or, at least, half listening. "Sure," she said. "Go on."

"Okay," Maria said. "Then she says, 'That's interesting that your mom is blind and has a Seeing Eye dog named Simba. I have a cousin who is deaf and has a hearing dog!'"

"Wow." Lizzie couldn't help being impressed. "That's cool. You'll have to ask her more about that."

Maria nodded and went on reading. "'Your family's cabin in the woods sounds cool. Who knows? Maybe someday if I visit you we could go there.'"

Lizzie felt another twinge. So far, she was the only friend Maria had brought to the cabin. The cabin was, like, *their* special place. "Are you almost ready to take Tank?" she asked. "He's about to pull my arm off."

"Okay," said Maria, quickly scanning through

the rest of the letter. "She just talks a little about how we seem to like the same books and movies and stuff. Then she signs off." She smiled as she folded the letter up, stuck it in her pocket, and took Tank's leash from Lizzie. "This is fun," she said. "I'm going to write her back today."

Maria chattered about her pen pal for the rest of the afternoon, until Lizzie was ready to scream. Who *cared* about Becky's dumb 4-H calf? Finally, they finished walking all the dogs and Lizzie headed home, wishing she'd never heard of this whole pen-pal thing.

"Hi, honey, we're in here," her mom called when she got home. Lizzie walked into the living room to find Mom talking to a tall, thin man. Rocky, snoring on his bed near the man's feet, barely opened one eye when Lizzie came in. "You remember Judge Thayer, don't you?" Mom asked. "We're just finishing up our interview."

Lizzie smiled at the judge. "Hi," she said.

Judge Thayer had a very dignified way about him, but he also had a kind smile. He stood up, then reached down to shake her hand. "Lizzie, right?" he asked.

She nodded.

"I've enjoyed meeting your newest foster pup," he told her as he sat back down. "Rocky is quite the clown — when he's awake."

Lizzie laughed. "Did he untie your shoes?" she asked. She'd learned over the past few days about a few more of Rocky's funny habits.

"Yes, that's quite a trick. Cocoa was smart, but she never did that." The judge chuckled and shook his head, reaching down to pet Rocky. He smiled wistfully. "If Cocoa had been this calm, we probably could have kept her," he murmured, almost to himself. "Too bad my wife, Charlotte, wouldn't consider any type of dog but a Lab."

Suddenly, Mom jumped up. "Oh, Lizzie," she said. "That reminds me. You got a letter today!" She pointed to the coffee table, and Lizzie saw an envelope there, covered in dog stickers.

# CHAPTER SEVEN

Lizzie snatched up the envelope. "It's from my pen pal!" There was her name, in the upper left-hand corner of the envelope: *Allyson Thatcher.*

Mom smiled. "I noticed that it's addressed to 'Lizzie Sarabeth Peterson,'" she said. "What's that all about?"

Lizzie waved a hand. "Nothing," she said. She stared at the envelope, noticing the special gold-trimmed dog stickers Allyson had used. She'd never seen those before. She loved the one of the Jack Russell terrier. It reminded her of Rascal, who was still one of her favorite foster puppies even though he had been a handful. Lizzie walked away, heading for her room. She couldn't wait to open Allyson's letter.

"Lizzie!" said her mother. "Aren't you going to say good-bye to Judge Thayer?"

Lizzie looked up to see her mother frowning at her. Oops. Maybe she had been a little rude. "Good-bye, Judge," she said. "It was nice to see you again."

Judge Thayer smiled understandingly. "Nice to see you, too," he said.

"And, Lizzie," her mother added, "I think Rocky needs to be taken outside before you go up to your room. And don't say Charles can do it. Dad and the boys are at the park with Buddy."

Lizzie let out a sigh. Normally she didn't mind taking care of their foster puppies. In fact, she loved it. But right *now*? When she had a letter to read? "He's sleeping!" she pointed out.

"Mmm-hmm," said Mom. "Guess you'll have to wake him up."

Exasperated, Lizzie went over to give Rocky a nudge. He woke with a snort and rolled over, paddling his paws and glancing around with a dazed look in his eyes. His mouth fell into an upside-down grin when he spotted Judge Thayer.

*Where am I? Oh, right. I fell asleep while that nice man was scratching my head.*

The judge burst out laughing, and so did Lizzie, in spite of her frustration. This puppy could make anyone laugh, no matter what mood they were in. "Come on, Rocky," she said. "Let's go out in the yard." Rocky scrambled to his feet and led Lizzie to the door. She smiled as she watched him go. His funny bowlegged walk was so cute.

Lizzie was dying to rip the letter open, but she made herself wait until Rocky was done in the backyard. When she brought him back in, he headed straight for his bed. Judge Thayer reached down a long, thin hand to pet him, and the solid little bulldog pup settled in with a contented sigh.

On her way upstairs, Lizzie opened the letter. It was written in purple marker that smelled like grapes and was decorated with more dog stickers and also drawings of dogs. Allyson was a good artist!

Just as she reached the top of the stairs, the phone rang. Lizzie went into her mom's study to answer it.

"Hey, Lizzie." It was Maria. "I just had a feeling that maybe you got a letter today. Did you?"

"Yes!" Lizzie yelled. She sat down on the twirly office chair.

"Cool!" said Maria. "What did Allyson have to say?"

"I haven't even read it yet," Lizzie said. "I'll read it to you now. 'Dear Lizzie,'" she read.

She skipped the part where Allyson wrote, "Or should I call you Sarabeth?"

Then she went on. "'It was great to get your letter. I'm so happy to have a pen pal! It can get pretty lonely out here on my family's ranch. We are forty miles from the nearest town.'"

"Wow," said Maria.

"I know," said Lizzie. "She really lives way out in the country. Anyway, then she says, 'I have two brothers, too. They are twins named Tinker and

Traven, and they are probably just as annoying as —'" Lizzie broke off. She did not want to read aloud the names that Allyson had written, Wolfgang and Sebastian. She glanced ahead and saw that Allyson talked about being jealous that Lizzie had a beautiful older sister. She also mentioned how cool it was that Lizzie's dad was the fire chief.

If Lizzie read those things out loud, Maria would know that she'd made up all kinds of silly stories when she wrote to her pen pal. Not lies, really. Just stories. But would Maria understand that?

"You know what?" she said into the phone. "I think I just want to read it myself first. Is that okay?"

"Sure," Maria said, after a second. Lizzie could tell she was wondering why Lizzie wouldn't read Allyson's letter out loud. After all, Maria had read Becky's letter out loud. But Maria had nothing to hide, and Lizzie did.

"Gotta go!" Lizzie said quickly, and hung up. Then she went into her own room and read through the whole letter. Allyson sounded so cool! She knew how to ride horses and rope calves, and she and her brothers were allowed to go camping by themselves in the wilderness, even though there were grizzly bears all over the place where she lived. She had four dogs and three cats and her own pony named Silver, and in the winter, when the snow was eight feet deep, she didn't have to go to school for weeks at a time.

Lizzie read Allyson's letter six more times that night, and once more before school the next morning. In class, when Mrs. Abeson asked if anyone else had gotten letters from their pen pals, Lizzie's hand was the first to shoot up. "I did!" she said.

"Wonderful," said her teacher. "Our project is really coming along. On Monday, I want everyone to bring in their letters so we can start making our bulletin board display. Won't it be fun to share our pen-pal experiences?"

# CHAPTER EIGHT

Lizzie's stomach lurched. What? Bring in their letters? Nobody had told her she was going to have to display the letter she had gotten from Allyson. How could she do that? If people read Allyson's letter, they'd find out that Lizzie had made up all sorts of things about herself. She clutched the sides of her desk and groaned.

"Are you okay?" Maria gave her a worried look.

Lizzie managed to nod. "Sure," she whispered. But she wasn't. For the rest of the school day, Lizzie worried. What was she going to do?

She was trapped. She had already raised her hand when Mrs. Abeson had asked who'd gotten letters, so she couldn't say that a letter had not come.

Maybe she could pretend to be sick on Monday, so she could stay at home. She had never done that before, but how hard could it be? She could just tell Mom that her stomach hurt. But that would only put things off for a day or two. Whenever she did come back to school, Mrs. Abeson would ask about the letter.

Could she say that her dog had eaten it? No, that was the oldest excuse in the book. Besides, she couldn't blame Buddy for doing something he would never do. And Rocky was not the chewing type, either.

Lizzie was in trouble, and she knew it was her own fault. Why hadn't she just told Allyson the truth about who she was? She needed help, and she knew it.

After school, she and Maria were in Maria's neighborhood, walking two dogs each. Lizzie held the tiny red leash of Pickle the Pomeranian in one hand and a hefty leather lead attached to a Lab mix named Tracker in the other. Maria was being towed along by twin poodles, Pogo and Pixie, who had enough energy for four dogs.

"What's the matter, anyway?" Maria asked. "You look like you're getting sick or something. Plus, you've been really quiet all day. That's not like you."

Lizzie hung her head. "I did something dumb," she admitted. "It was just for fun, but now . . . ugh. Now I don't know what to do."

Maria just looked at her. "Go on," she said.

Lizzie knew what her friend was probably

thinking. This was not the first time Lizzie had gotten herself into a jam. "You know that letter I got from Allyson?" she asked. "Well, there's no way I can bring it in and pin it up on the bulletin board in class."

"Why not?" asked Maria.

Lizzie sighed. "Well, I sort of made some things up when I wrote to Allyson. Stuff about my life. I was just trying to make myself sound more interesting, so she'd like me."

Maria looked shocked. "You mean, you lied?"

Lizzie squirmed. "I didn't *lie* exactly." But even as she said it, she knew that she *had* lied. She had not told the truth, and even though she hadn't done it to hurt anybody, it was still a lie. "Okay, so maybe I did," she said. "But let's forget about that for a minute. The problem is, when she wrote me back she said things in her letter that make it obvious that I . . . lied. I can't put her letter up on the bulletin board. The question is, what do I do about it?"

Maria opened her mouth and shut it again without saying anything. Then Pogo and Pixie dragged her off to one side so they could smell an especially interesting mailbox.

Lizzie smiled sadly down at Pickle. "Think she'll help me?" she whispered to the tiny dog. Pickle sat up on her hind legs and put one tiny paw on Lizzie's leg. That meant she wanted to be carried for a while. Pickle was a little spoiled.

Maria did not say much until they had finished walking all the dogs, even Ginger and Rocky. When they were done, they went to Lizzie's house, grabbed an apple each from the bowl on the kitchen counter, and went up to her room. Lizzie sat on the bed with Rocky on her lap, and Maria sat on the floor, playing tug with Buddy.

"Okay," Maria said finally. "Here's what I think. You were a dope to lie to Allyson."

"I know." Lizzie looked down at the letter in her hands. Allyson's letter. She had gotten it out to show to Maria.

"I mean," Maria went on, "you're pretty cool just the way you are. And so's your family. Who needs a beautiful older sister, anyway?" She leaned over to tickle Lizzie's foot.

"I know," Lizzie said again, although deep inside she still thought it had been kind of fun to make up a pretend sister.

"Let's see that letter again," said Maria.

Lizzie handed it over and waited while Maria read through it. Rocky had fallen asleep on her lap and was snoring peacefully. Lizzie could tell that even a short walk had been plenty for him.

Rocky was so different from Cocoa. The chocolate Lab pup had needed as much exercise as you could give her, and still she never seemed to get tired. Lizzie petted Rocky's short, smooth coat. That was the interesting thing about fostering dogs, she thought. Each one was so different.

"The answer's right here!" Maria said, tapping the letter with her finger.

"Where?" Lizzie asked.

"See, at the end here, after 'Sincerely, Allyson'?" Maria held up the letter and pointed. "She put her e-mail address. All you have to do is write her a note explaining what happened. Then she can e-mail you back a new letter and you can print it out and bring it to school on Monday."

Lizzie grinned. "You're a genius!" she said. Then her smile faded. "Except for one thing," she said. "I'm going to have to tell Allyson the truth."

# CHAPTER NINE

"Come on," Maria said. "You can do it."

Lizzie sighed. It was going to be so embarrassing to have to explain things to her pen pal. But it would be even more embarrassing to bring Allyson's letter to school and pin it up. How would she explain it? Everybody knew her brothers were named Charles and the Bean, not Sebastian and Wolfgang.

There was no getting around it. "Okay, Rocky," Lizzie said, kissing the bulldog's wrinkly face. "You're going to have to get off my lap so I can write an e-mail."

Rocky woke with a snort and climbed down onto the floor, stretching and yawning.

*Aaah, there's nothing like a good nap. So refreshing!*

Then he rolled over onto his back and paddled his paws at Buddy, inviting him to play.

Lizzie and Maria laughed. "What a clown," said Maria. "He'd cheer anybody up."

Rocky followed them down the hall to Mom's study and Lizzie logged on. She sat there for a minute, trying to figure out what to say to Allyson.

"'Dear Allyson,'" Maria suggested. "'I have a confession to make. . . .'"

A few minutes later, Lizzie had finished writing. She copied over her original letter to Allyson, the one where she had told the truth, and added that to her confession. Then she hit "send." With luck, Allyson would A) forgive her for making up stories, and B) write her a new letter in time for Lizzie to bring it in to class on Monday morning.

Lizzie spun around on the chair. "Thanks," she said to Maria. Actually, it was a relief to set the record straight. Lizzie had felt a little funny about that first letter she had sent to Allyson. "Hey, you know what I was thinking?" she asked. "It hit me when you said that I'm pretty cool the way I am. Well, so is Rocky."

"So is Rocky?" Maria asked, looking confused.

Lizzie sat down on the floor and pulled the stocky bulldog pup onto her lap. "Rocky is pretty cool just the way he is," she explained. "So what if he's not a guard dog? So what if he'll never win the blue ribbon at an agility trial? He's Rocky. He's funny and sweet and really easy to take care of. He doesn't bark or jump on people, and he hardly needs any exercise. And he makes everybody smile and laugh."

Maria nodded. "You're right," she said. She reached out to pet Rocky's smooth coat. "He's the perfect dog for *somebody*."

"And all we have to do is figure out who that somebody is," Lizzie said thoughtfully.

*Bing!* The computer made a noise that made both girls jump. Lizzie spun back around on the chair and stared at the screen. Allyson's name had popped up. "She wrote back already!" Lizzie said. "She must have been online and read my letter right away." She sat down in the office chair and clicked on Allyson's note.

"What did she say?" Maria asked.

Lizzie laughed. "You're not going to believe this," she said. "Allyson lied, too!"

"You're kidding," said Maria.

"No, listen to this. She says she couldn't stand to tell me the real truth about her boring life after she read my exciting letter. So she made a few things up." Lizzie spun around in the chair. "My pen pal and I seem to have a lot in common, too!" she said, grinning at Maria.

Maria giggled. "So, what did she make up?" she asked. "Does she really live on a ranch?"

"She does." Lizzie read as quickly as she could. "But it's only a few acres, and they just have one cow. She does have two brothers, but they're not twins and their names are Steven and Jason. She doesn't have a pony. She never saw a grizzly bear, although some people around there have seen them up in the mountains. And instead of four dogs and three cats, they have one kitten and an old hound dog."

Lizzie swallowed. Allyson was not quite as exciting as she'd first seemed. She didn't even know how to ride and rope like a real cowgirl, though she said she wanted to learn.

By now, Maria was reading over her shoulder. "She sounds really, really nice," she said. "And she said she'd write you another letter to bring to school."

Lizzie nodded. She still felt disappointed. It wasn't really fair to feel that way, since she had made up stuff about herself, too. But she had been hoping for an extra-cool pen pal. Now she just had a regular one, sort of like Maria's pen pal, Becky. At least Allyson lived in Montana. That counted for something, didn't it?

Rocky ambled over in his bowlegged way and put his paw up on Lizzie's knee.

*Things are getting kind of serious in here. What's the big deal? How about some smiles?*

Lizzie grinned at him and scratched his head. "Well, Rocky. I guess you and I — and Allyson — aren't the most exciting folks in the world. But that's okay. We're still pretty cool, once you get to know us. Right?"

Rocky looked up at her and panted a happy huff. He wagged his little stub of a tail and blinked his big, sparkly eyes.

Then Mom walked in. "Okay, girls, time to finish up here. I need the computer so I can get my last article done. I promised Judge Thayer he could read his interview before I sent it in to my editor." She looked at Lizzie. "Maybe you and Maria could drop it off at his place tomorrow when you're out walking Ginger and

Rocky. He lives just a few blocks from Ginger's home."

Lizzie nodded. "Sure," she said. Then she remembered the way the judge had smiled when he looked at Rocky. She poked Maria. "Hey," she said. "I think I have an idea."

# CHAPTER TEN

The next morning at school, Lizzie stood near the bulletin board, waiting her turn to pin up her pen-pal letter. Nobody but Maria would ever know that it was not the *first* letter she had gotten from Allyson. Since she and Allyson had some of the exact same dog stickers, Lizzie had put a few of her own onto the e-mail she had printed out — so it even looked like a real letter.

She was proud to pin it up. Allyson sounded funny and cool, and her life in Montana was definitely different from Lizzie's life. When it was her turn, Lizzie took four red pushpins and stuck her letter right in the middle of the board. She turned to see Maria watching her, and she grinned at her friend. Maria smiled back. Lizzie felt grateful to Maria for helping her out of a jam. Maria was the best friend she could ever have.

She watched Maria pin up Becky's letter. Then the two of them linked arms and headed back to their seats, whispering about the plan they'd made for Rocky's future.

It was so obvious. The day before, Lizzie had realized that Rocky would be perfect for Judge Thayer and his wife, Charlotte. They'd had to give up Cocoa, the chocolate Lab, because she just had too much energy for them to deal with. But, as Lizzie had told Maria, that didn't mean they couldn't have a dog at all. And what better dog than Rocky, who hardly needed any exercise? Plus, he was such a clown. He would keep them laughing every day. It was a perfect match.

Except for one thing — the thing Lizzie had remembered that morning, as she was brushing her teeth.

"All we have to do is prove to Mrs. Thayer that she could love a bulldog," Lizzie told Maria now. "Judge Thayer said his wife wouldn't even consider a dog that wasn't a Lab."

"But who wouldn't fall in love with Rocky right away?" Maria asked.

"Exactly," said Lizzie. "That's why we're going to make sure that Rocky and Charlotte Thayer meet each other — today."

Later that afternoon, when Maria and Lizzie finished walking all their other clients' dogs, they stopped at Lizzie's house to pick up Rocky. Mom handed Lizzie a big brown envelope. "Judge Thayer is expecting you," she said.

Lizzie couldn't wait to get to the judge's house.

She tried to hurry Rocky along, but it was no use. He trundled along in his usual poky way, sniffing at everything and stopping once in a while for a happy, squirming roll in the grass.

It got even worse when they picked up Ginger. Now they had *two* slowpoke dogs on their hands. Lizzie was so impatient that she began hopping from foot to foot as she waited for the dogs to sniff. "Take it easy," Maria told Lizzie. "We'll get there."

Finally, they did. Lizzie double-checked the house number. "This is it," she announced. The judge lived in a small light-blue house, nothing fancy. Lizzie had expected a judge to live in something a little more . . . important. But it was a cute house, and there was a fenced-in yard, which was always a good thing for dog owners, and a pretty little garden all blooming with yellow and purple flowers.

Lizzie opened the front gate, and she and Maria — and Rocky and Ginger — walked up to the porch. "Sit, Rocky," said Lizzie, as she rang the bell. She wanted him on his best behavior.

Judge Thayer smiled when he opened the door. "Well, well, well," he said. "Hello, Lizzie."

"Hi," said Lizzie. "This is my best friend, Maria."

Judge Thayer reached down to shake Maria's hand. He was so formal! Even in the middle of the afternoon, he wore a suit and tie and a crisp white shirt. Then he bent over to pet Rocky. "And I believe this charming young man and I have already met," he said. "Hello there, Rocky."

Rocky squirmed and snorted happily.

"And this is Ginger," Maria said.

"A pleasure to meet you, young lady," said the judge, shaking Ginger's paw. Ginger looked a lit-tle confused, but she wagged her tail.

When he straightened up, Lizzie handed Judge Thayer the envelope. "Here's the interview," she said. "Mom says you have two days to look it over. Then she has to turn it in."

"I'm sure it will be just fine," said the judge. "Your mother is a talented journalist." He smiled at Lizzie. "Thank you for bringing it over."

He looked as if he were ready to say good-bye.

"Um, is your wife home?" Lizzie blurted out. She wasn't sure how else to ask.

Judge Thayer shook his head. "Charlotte is off at the grocery store," he said. "I know she'll be sorry to have missed you."

Not as sorry as Lizzie was. Lizzie looked down at Rocky. If only Charlotte Thayer could meet him! "I was kind of hoping..." she began. Just then, a silver car pulled into the driveway.

"There she is now," said the judge. "Let's help her unload her purchases, shall we?" He led the girls and the dogs over to the car. Charlotte looked surprised when she opened the door and climbed out. She was a small woman who always reminded Lizzie of a bright-eyed little bird.

"Land sakes, Ernest," she said. "Who have you got here?"

Judge Thayer introduced the girls. "You remember Lizzie, don't you?" he asked. "She and her family took care of Cocoa when I hurt my ankle."

A shadow seemed to pass over Charlotte Thayer's face at the mention of Cocoa. Lizzie could tell that she must still miss the beautiful chocolate Lab very much. But she smiled at Lizzie. "Of course. And who might these creatures be?" she asked, peering at Ginger and Rocky.

"This is Ginger," said Maria. "We have a dog-walking business, and she's one of our clients."

"And this," Lizzie said, "is another puppy my family is fostering. We're looking for a perfect forever home for him. His name is Rocky." At the sound of his name Rocky sat up, panting his happy huff. He held up a paw and smiled his bulldog smile.

*That's me! Rocky's my name, clowning is my game.*

Charlotte Thayer's eyes brightened. "Why, what a funny little darling," she said. She reached down to pet Rocky.

"He is funny," said Lizzie. "And he hardly needs any exercise at all! He's a real couch potato. He doesn't bark, or drool, or jump up on people. All he wants is to be loved."

"Hmm," said Charlotte.

"Can we help bring in your groceries?" Lizzie asked. She winked at Maria, to let her know it was all part of the plan. She wanted Mrs. Thayer to have a few minutes to get to know Rocky.

"I'll show you where to put them," said Judge Thayer. Lizzie had a feeling he'd noticed her wink and knew exactly what she was up to. Sure enough, he gave *her* a wink as he handed her a sack of groceries. "Why don't you just relax out here and keep an eye on the dogs?" he said to Charlotte.

By the time the girls and Judge Thayer came back outside, Charlotte was perched on the back steps, scratching Rocky between the ears. Rocky grunted happily and looked up at her with a silly bulldog smile. Then he rolled over and paddled his paws, and his upside-down smile grew even wider.

Judge Thayer burst out laughing.

Charlotte looked surprised. She glanced up at her husband. "Ernest, I believe that's the first time I've heard you laugh like that since we had to give up Cocoa."

Judge Thayer sat down next to Charlotte and took his wife's hand. "That's way too long to go without a good laugh," he said.

Charlotte leaned against him and smiled. "I know I said I couldn't imagine having any dog if I couldn't have a Lab. But this fellow is something special. I believe he'd keep us both in stitches every day. What do you think, Ernest? Could we give this silly boy a home?"

The judge didn't answer. He just knelt right down on the grass, in his good suit, and threw his arms around Rocky. "What do you say, buddy?" he asked.

Rocky rolled over, jumped up, and barked happily as he wagged his stubby little tail.

*Sounds great to me!*

Lizzie and Maria looked at each other and smiled. Rocky had found a forever home with people who would love him just as he was. What could be better than that?

# PUPPY TIPS

Rocky's first owner got him because he wanted a guard dog, but as Lizzie knew, that's not what bulldogs are best at. If your family is thinking about getting a dog, it's a good idea to learn about different breeds and figure out which one will suit your family best. Do you like to spend lots of time outdoors, the way I do? Not all dogs love hiking and swimming, but an athletic Lab or a German shepherd would be a good choice. If you live in a city apartment, a smaller, less athletic dog like a Pomeranian or Chihuahua might make more sense. Take the time to find the perfect dog for your family, and both you and the dog will be much happier.

Dear Reader,

I never had an official pen pal, but I love to read and write letters. When I was your age, there was no e-mail or texting so my friends and I wrote letters to each other whenever we were apart. I still have some letters I got from my friend Sophie when we were in fourth grade and she was away for the summer!

I wish I could be pen pals with all my fans and readers, but if I did that, I'd spend *all* my time writing letters and I wouldn't be able to write books! If you're interested in having a pen pal, ask your parents to help you find a pen-pal site online.

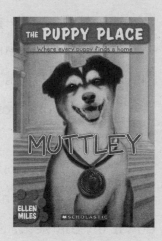

Happy writing!
Ellen Miles

P.S. If you want to read about another puppy who isn't as sleepy as he seems, try MUTTLEY.

## DON'T MISS THE
## NEXT PUPPY PLACE
## ADVENTURE!

**Here's a peek at** LUCY!

"We're stopping to pick up Aunt Amanda on our way," Dad told Charles, as they backed out of the driveway in Dad's red pickup. "I heard about the puppy from her, and she insists on coming with us."

"What kind of puppy is it? Where did it come from? Is it a boy or a girl?" Charles bounced up and down on his seat. Already, he'd almost forgotten all about his bad day. How bad a day could it be if they were getting a new puppy to foster?

Dad smiled. "I really don't have many details," he said. "The only question I can answer is where the dog came from. Remember how we heard about all that flooding down south last week? Lots of pets were left homeless when people's houses washed away. The shelters down there have done everything they can to find each dog's family, but there are still some animals left needing homes."

"But how did the puppy get up here?" Charles asked.

"Aunt Amanda has an old friend named Bunny who runs an all-breed rescue," Dad said. "She takes in all kinds of dogs and tries to find them homes, just the way we take in puppies. Her place is sort of a cross between a foster home and a shelter. I guess she has so many dogs right now that she just can't handle one more, especially a young one. When Aunt Amanda told her that we foster puppies, she couldn't wait to meet us."

Charles sat quietly for a moment, imagining what kind of puppy they would be meeting. Maybe it would be a cute little Pomeranian. He'd always wanted to foster one of those. Or maybe it was a larger breed. Charles had loved Maggie, the huge Saint Bernard puppy his family had fostered.

"You okay, pal?" Dad broke the silence while they waited at a stoplight. "You looked pretty bummed out when you first came home. Want to talk about it?"

Charles shrugged. "I just had a bad day, that's all. I messed up in a kickball game, and Sammy teased me about something, and stuff like that." He played with the buckle on his seatbelt.

Dad nodded. "Not every day can be a winner, I guess." He shook his head. "That Sammy sure does like to joke around. I bet he didn't mean to hurt your feelings."

Charles looked out the window. He didn't want to talk about it anymore. He just wanted to forget about his bad day.

# ABOUT THE AUTHOR

Ellen Miles loves dogs, which is why she has a great time writing the Puppy Place books. And guess what? She loves cats, too! (In fact, her very first pet was a beautiful tortoiseshell cat named Jenny.) That's why she came up with a brand-new series called Kitty Corner. Ellen lives in Vermont and loves to be outdoors every day, walking, biking, skiing, or swimming, depending on the season. She also loves to read, cook, explore her beautiful state, play with dogs, and hang out with friends and family.

Visit Ellen at www.ellenmiles.net.